ORCA
YOUNG
READERS

MURPHY
and Mousetrap

Sylvia Olsen

ORCA BOOK PUBLISHERS

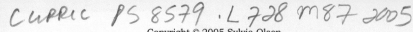

Copyright © 2005 Sylvia Olsen

National Library of Canada Cataloguing in Publication Data:

Olsen, Sylvia, 1955-
Murphy and Mousetrap / Sylvia Olsen.

(Orca young readers)
ISBN 1-55143-344-3

I. Title. II. Series.

PS8579.L728M87 2005   jC813'.6   C2005-901127-0

First published in the United States 2005\

Library of Congress Control Number: 2005922035

Summary: When Murphy, his mother and their cat Mousetrap move back to the reserve, Murphy is sure that both he and the cat are going to be miserable.

Free teachers' guide available. www.orcabook.com

Orca Book Publishers gratefully acknowledges the support for its publishing programs provided by the following agencies: the Government of Canada through the Department of Canadian Heritage's Book Publishing Industry Development Program (BPIDP), the Canada Council for the Arts, and the British Columbia Arts Council.

Cover Design and typesetting: Lynn O'Rourke
Cover & interior illustrations by Darlene Gait

In Canada:
Orca Book Publishers
Box 5626 Stn. B
Victoria, BC Canada
V8R 6S4

In the United States:
Orca Book Publishers
PO Box 468
Custer, WA USA
98240-0468

08 07 06 05 • 5 4 3 2 1

Printed and bound in Canada

For Adam

1

Murphy plunked his schoolbag on the hall floor and stuck his hand in his pocket. He rummaged through the stones he had picked up on the way home from school until he felt the apartment key on its loop of string. Mom had made him promise to wear the key around his neck so it wouldn't get lost, but it tickled when it hung against his body. And it strangled him when he pulled his sweatshirt over his head, so he had stuffed the key in his pocket.

He slid the key into the lock and jiggled it back and forth until the door opened.

"Hey, Mousetrap, I'm home," Murphy called.

He walked through the living room to his bedroom and threw his coat and bag on the bed.

"Mousetrap, where are you?" Murphy said. He placed his hands on his hips like Mom did when she really meant what she was saying.

"I'm coming," he called.

He kicked off his shoes and walked softly on his toes.

"I'll find you."

Each afternoon after school Murphy and Mousetrap played the same game. As soon as Mousetrap heard Murphy open the door he ran to one of his favorite hiding spots. When Murphy called, the cat stayed perfectly still. Every afternoon Murphy stood in the living room, hands on his hips, acting as mad as he could muster. Then he tiptoed from room to room, peeking in corners and closets and cupboards.

"I'm coming, ready or not," Murphy said in his sternest voice. He slipped into the bathroom, pulled back the shower curtain and peeked into the bathtub. It was empty.

He tiptoed back into his bedroom, lifted the corner of his bedspread and peeked under the bed. He checked around the books stacked under the computer table and glanced behind the computer monitor: that was Mousetrap's favorite sleeping spot. He loved to lie next to the warm screen, but Murphy had a feeling he wouldn't be there when the computer was turned off.

"You little sneak," Murphy called out. Sometimes, like today, Mousetrap picked such a good hiding spot that Murphy had trouble finding him. Although Murphy liked the game, he got a lump in his throat when, after a few minutes, he couldn't find his cat. He worried that one day Mousetrap might not be there. Could Mousetrap have found a way out of the apartment? Could he have climbed out the window and wandered off?

"Come on, Mousetrap!" Murphy called. This time he had a quiver in his voice. "I know you're here."

Mom's room was next. As he entered, he thought he saw the edge of the bedspread twitch slightly. Murphy tiptoed across the floor and lifted the bedspread. Mousetrap's thick fluffy white tail sprang out from under the bed. Murphy dropped to his knees and gathered up his cat.

"I got you," he said. He buried his face in the furry ball. "Good hiding spot."

Mousetrap was just as happy as Murphy when he was finally found. He rubbed his soft face against Murphy's cheek and climbed up onto his shoulders. He curled around Murphy's neck and hung on as Murphy went into the kitchen and made a peanut-butter-and-jam sandwich. When Murphy was finished he sat down at his computer to scan the Internet for Web sites that would describe the stone he had found on the way home from school. Mousetrap stepped off his shoulders, crept across the keyboard and tucked himself into his favorite spot beside the computer screen.

Murphy dug in his pockets and pulled out a handful of stones. Dirt, leaves and sand spilled onto the floor as he laid the stones in a row on the computer desk. Most of the stones were gray, or gray and black or white.

But when he had passed the park that afternoon he had wandered up the path instead of staying right on the sidewalk as he had promised. Out of the corner of his eye, Murphy had glimpsed a dark green stone unlike anything he had ever seen. It was wedged in tight next to a rock outcropping. After he pried it out, spat on it and rubbed it against his pant leg, the stone glistened like a marble.

Mousetrap lay in a sleepy pile with his eyes open just enough to watch Murphy place the stones into a pile.

"So, Mousetrap," Murphy said, passing the small green stone in front of his cat's half-open eyes. "What kind of stone do you think this is?"

Mousetrap's ears shot up and he opened his blue eyes wide. His tail was curled around his body, and the tip rested under his chin. It twitched as he examined the stone.

Murphy waited patiently as if Mousetrap would identify the stone, before he placed it next to others. Soon Murphy had three piles. Each pile contained similar stones. Mousetrap and Murphy examined the stones and the Web sites until they heard the key turn in the front door. Then Murphy grabbed Mousetrap and ran into the bathroom. He jumped into the bathtub and pulled the shower curtain around them. He tucked his cat onto his lap, took a deep breath and held on until he heard the door open.

"Murphy, I'm home," Mom called.

She shut the door and walked through the hall to the kitchen. Murphy heard plastic bags drop on to the kitchen floor and then a shuffle, which was probably Mom taking off her coat and throwing it over a kitchen chair.

"Mousetrap," Mom called. "Where are you?"

Murphy didn't move, and Mousetrap stayed perfectly still. Murphy imagined Mom standing in the living room with her hands on her hips.

The living room floor creaked as she stepped toward Murphy's bedroom.

"Murphy, I know you're here."

Her steps moved into her own bedroom, and Murphy heard her open the closet and say, "Where are you two?"

Her footsteps got louder and louder. Murphy caught another breath and squeezed

Mousetrap. Just as he was about to jump out to surprise her, Mom pulled back the shower curtain.

"Gotcha!" she cried. She pulled Murphy and Mousetrap out of the bathtub, hugged her son and stroked Mousetrap on the head.

"You scared me," Murphy said.

"You scared me too," Mom said with a laugh.

Murphy had lived with Mom and Mousetrap in the apartment for as long as he could remember. His dad lived in another city in another province. Murphy didn't know much about his dad except that Mom said Dad left him three things: his blue eyes, which weren't like Mom's at all, his blond hair and his name, Murphy. Mom had decided to call her son Murphy Jones: Dad's last name first, Murphy, and Mom's last name second, Jones. That was just about all Murphy knew about his dad.

His dad had left before he was born, so it had always just been the three of them. Mom said Murphy was only two months old when neighbors down the hall moved out and left

Mousetrap behind. When Mom came home from work, Mousetrap, who was just a little kitten at the time, was wandering up and down the hall. Mom picked him up and took him home. He was a tiny ball of white fluff. Mom said he looked like a snowball, his hair sparkled so much. Mom figured Mousetrap and Murphy must have been almost the same age, so they both celebrated their ninth birthday on October 30.

Murphy knew that cat years made Mousetrap much older even though they were both born at the same time. That didn't make much sense to Murphy, but most of the time Mousetrap did act like an old cat. He preferred to lie around the house curled into a tight ball fast asleep. Sometimes Mousetrap played with Murphy, games like hide-and-seek. But he didn't run around like he did when he was younger or play with invisible things or jump at things that Murphy couldn't see.

"Murphy, come and set the table," Mom called.

Supper was hot and steamy on the stove and smelled like fried salmon, Murphy and

Mousetrap's favorite. Mousetrap stayed at Murphy's heels as Murphy walked back and forth with plates and knives and forks. Then the cat jumped up onto a chair and watched expectantly as Mom placed fish and potatoes next to the butter and salt and pepper.

"Mmmm," Murphy said as he sat down. "Supper looks good."

2

"How was your day at school?" Mom asked. She sat at one end of the table, and Murphy sat at the other. The window was between them on one side, and Mousetrap sat on the chair opposite the window.

"Good," Murphy said. He plopped a pile of mashed potatoes next to his fish. "Real good."

After he smoothed out a gully in the top of the potatoes and filled it with soft butter, he said, "I found a really cool green stone on the way home."

Mom said, "Great," and then she added, "I got a new job today."

"Oh, yeah?"

Murphy didn't know much about the work Mom did. He knew Mom left early in the morning and arrived home in time to make supper. Except Saturday and Sunday. Those days they spent together. The other thing Murphy knew was Mom's job never paid quite enough money to buy everything they needed. Sometimes Mom couldn't afford to pay the phone bill if she talked too much long distance. Other times she didn't have enough money to buy milk for the whole week, and by Friday Murphy had to eat toast and jam instead of cereal for breakfast.

"I'll make a lot more money, and we'll get to move home."

"That's good," Murphy said. Mom would be happy if she had enough money to take him to a movie or out for lunch.

He pulled a strip of salmon off his plate, checked for bones and tossed it on the chair in front of Mousetrap. Mousetrap rubbed his pink nose into the fish and lapped it happily into his mouth.

"What do you mean, we'll get to move home?" Murphy asked.

"With Grandma." Murphy could tell from the look on Mom's face that she was happy about moving and her new job. "We're going to move back to the reserve. To Grandma's place up island where I lived when I was a kid."

Murphy remembered Grandma's house. He had visited in the summer. When he got there his cousins had chased him around the field and up the street until he ran into the house and hid in the bathroom. He ended up sitting next to Mom almost the whole day while she talked to Grandma, Auntie Jean and Uncle Charlie.

When Mom told him to go out and play with Albert and Danny, he said he wasn't feeling well. It was true. He wasn't feeling well, and the more he thought about playing with the boys, the worse he felt. They came in once or twice and said, "Come on, Murphy. We're gonna play soccer," but he could tell from the sound of their voices that playing soccer with them wouldn't be safe.

Mom called Grandma's place the Indian reserve. Sometimes she called it the First Nation, but she never called it home. Grandma's place wasn't home. Not for Murphy.

"This is our home," Murphy said.

"But we'll get to live with my family," Mom said. "You'll love it."

"We're family," Murphy said. "You, me and Mousetrap."

Mom wasn't thinking the same way as Murphy, and he didn't like what she said.

"There'll be other boys around. You won't be so lonely, all on your own. And there'll be your aunties and uncles."

"I'm not lonely," Murphy said. "This is home. I have you and Mousetrap."

Why did Mom have to talk about moving home? They had a perfectly good home.

He looked around the kitchen. His drawings and paintings covered one wall—some he had done as long ago as kindergarten. Fridge magnets held up photos of Mom and Mousetrap and Murphy and photos of the camping trip with Bernie and Chas, Mom's best friends. Murphy thought about when he helped Mom cut the curtain to fit the kitchen window, and how he had chosen the kitchen wallpaper himself—colorful blue and green airplanes.

Grandma's place wasn't anything like the apartment. When Murphy traveled up the island to visit Grandma there were always a lot of people around the house. They might be his aunties and uncles, but he didn't know them.

Murphy only talked to Grandma on the phone once in a while. Whenever Murphy overheard phone conversations between Mom and her sisters, who lived on the reserve, Mom always said she liked being in the city and living in the apartment.

"You said you didn't want to live on the Indian reserve," Murphy said. "You don't even talk to your family. Hardly ever."

"I've been talking to Grandma a lot lately. She wants me to move home. And our First Nation offered me a good job," Mom said.

Mousetrap had curled up in a ball on the chair and tucked his face under the tip of his tail. He was full of salmon and pleased as he could be.

"We'll have an apartment in Grandma's basement. Just for us. It's all ready."

Murphy didn't know what the Indian reserve was except that's where Grandma lived. All the houses around Grandma's place belonged to his aunties and uncles, and Mom said all the kids were his cousins. There were no apartment buildings, gas stations, streetlights or sidewalks. There was no McDonalds. There wasn't even a school nearby. There were plenty of houses. Most of them looked old and were placed higgledy-piggledy off to the side of the road, not lined up straight like they were in the city. There were fields and bushes and mountains that were far too high for Murphy to climb. And there was a long sandy beach with millions of brightly colored stones.

When Murphy thought about the stones he felt a little bit excited. There would be more than stones for his collection. Murphy remembered Mom telling him that if he turned the stones over he could find glass trade beads and arrowheads that his great-grandparents had used.

Everyone around Grandma's house was

First Nation. That was the part that worried Murphy. He didn't look anything like the people on the reserve. Mom said if someone looked closely they could tell Murphy was First Nation. At least half-First Nation. She said he looked like her. They had the same big round eyes and thick hair, except everything about Murphy was light, and everything about Mom was dark. Especially Murphy's skin. It was so white it burned beet-red in the summer if he wasn't careful. "Pale skin. That's another thing his dad left him," Murphy had over-heard Mom say to Chas.

Murphy put down his fork and squished his fists into his eyes. They felt hot and stingy like tears would burst out if he didn't stop them. Finally he looked up at Mom.

He rubbed the tickle out of his nose and asked, "What about Mousetrap?"

"He'll come with us," Mom said. "Of course. We wouldn't leave him behind." She reached over and stroked Mousetrap's head.

It wasn't the idea of leaving Mousetrap behind that worried Murphy; it was the memory of the cats he had seen around Grandma's place.

Cats on the reserve didn't look like Mousetrap. They weren't fat and fluffy like they slept on velvet pillows. They were lean, with hungry looks on their faces. They didn't seem like they were stuffed with salmon. There wasn't one pure white cat, not one with silky white hair and not a spot of another color on its body, not on the reserve.

"What if Mousetrap doesn't want to move?" Murphy asked.

Mom laughed.

It wasn't funny. Murphy knew that given the choice Mousetrap would stay right where they were. And Murphy agreed with his cat.

"Mousetrap will love it," Mom said. "You wait, Murphy, both of you will love it."

After supper, Murphy loaded the dishwasher and went into his bedroom. He gathered the piles of stones he had left by his computer and put them away neatly into the cardboard boxes he used to store his collection. He shut down his computer and climbed into bed. Mousetrap jumped up beside him. Murphy shut his eyes tight and listened for the low rumbling purr from deep in Mousetrap's belly.

3

"February first," Mom said. "Only four weeks until we have to be out of this apartment."

She dragged boxes home from the grocery store and piled them in each room. She pulled blankets, old clothes and books from shelves and closets and folded them neatly in the boxes. When a box was full, she taped it closed and wrote boldly with felt pen on the top: MURPHY'S CLOTHES or BOOKS or BLANKETS or SHOES.

The apartment didn't feel like home after Mom started packing. Mousetrap crept around the giant cardboard towers, and Murphy tried to ignore them. He didn't want to play hide-and-seek after school anymore, and Mom didn't

19

have time to play anything. One week before they had to leave the apartment, Bernie and Chas drove into the parking lot in a big green pickup truck.

Murphy stood at the door of the apartment with Mousetrap wrapped in his arms watching Mom and Bernie and Chas carry out box after box after box.

"We're just leaving the stuff we'll need in the next week," Mom said.

They left the beds, the sofa and the kitchen table and chairs. The bathroom closet was empty except for the tooth-brushes and a few containers of Mom's things. Two plates, two glasses and two bowls sat in the kitchen cabinet. The only thing left in Murphy's room was a laundry hamper next to his bed with a few pairs of socks, underwear, jeans and a couple of T-shirts. Even his dresser had been packed in the truck.

"Are you sure you want to do this?" Chas said to Mom once the truck was loaded. Chas and Bernie lived in the apartment across the street from Mom and Murphy. They had been

Mom's best friends for as long as Murphy could remember.

Mom slumped forward. "It's kind of late to be asking that now, don't you think?" she said. Chas put her arms around Mom's shoulders.

"But we're going to miss you," Chas said.

"I have to go," Mom insisted. "Don't make me cry. It's an opportunity for me. I won't get a job offer like this again."

"I know, I know," Chas said.

"I have to, Chas," Mom threw her arms around her friend.

"Quit it, you girls," Bernie said. "We're only going up for the day. We'll be right back."

Mom checked the boxes piled in the back of the truck, nodded and said, "We'll follow behind in my car and meet you there."

"Come on, Murphy," Mom said. "Time to go."

Murphy's chin drooped. His hands gripped Mousetrap firmly.

"You better put Mousetrap back in the apartment," Mom said. "He won't want to drive all that way."

Murphy turned back to the empty apartment. "He doesn't want to stay home," Murphy said. "How about if I stay home with him?"

"Grandma's expecting us," Mom said. "She's cooking supper."

Mousetrap curled his paws around Murphy's wrists. Murphy knew Mousetrap didn't want to ride all the way to Grandma's. It would take three hours to get there and three hours to get home. But Mousetrap wouldn't want to stay home either, not in an empty apartment, or a nearly empty apartment, all by himself.

"We'll be okay here," Murphy said. "Bernie and Chas can eat Grandma's supper. And you."

He dipped his nose into the soft belly of his cat. How would Mousetrap be sure they were coming back?

"Take him back inside, Murphy," Mom said. "And hurry up. We have to go."

Mom's words were sharp. She was tired. It wasn't a good time to argue with her.

"Then let's take him with us. He won't mind the drive." Murphy knew his words weren't true. Mousetrap hated the car.

"You know he doesn't like being in the car," Mom said. "Last time he threw up in the back seat."

And it stank. After Mousetrap's last ride, the car had a sickly smell for months even though Mom had scrubbed and scrubbed.

Mom was right. Murphy couldn't stay home, and Mousetrap couldn't come. Murphy trudged back into the apartment. He entered his bedroom. The bed looked the same as ever. Mom hadn't pulled the sheets and blankets off yet. Murphy leaned forward to place Mousetrap on the bed, but the cat curled his paws around Murphy's arm.

"Mousetrap, you have to stay here," Murphy pleaded.

He shook his arm until his cat dropped onto the bed. Murphy lay down beside him and stroked his soft belly. "I'll be back in a few hours," he said. "You'll be okay."

Mousetrap lay on the pillow and closed his eyes.

"I'll be back," Murphy said. "I promise."

Murphy stayed for a few moments until he could hear the deep sounds of his cat sleeping. Then he left the apartment, making sure he locked the door behind him.

"Hurry up, Murphy," Mom called as he neared the car.

Murphy crawled into the front seat and buckled his seat belt. He curled his body into a ball and thought about Mousetrap. Would his cat think they had abandoned him altogether? Did Mousetrap know they were coming back real soon?

"We'll be back in a few hours," Mom said. "Don't worry. We leave him alone every day when we go to school and to work."

"Yeah," Murphy said. But Mom didn't understand Mousetrap. She thought he was just a normal cat.

4

Chugga. Chugga. Chugga.

Mom stepped on the gas when they reached the long hill that climbed into the mountains. Their car got slower and slower while other cars whizzed past them.

"Oh gawd, Murphy," she moaned. "This old girl is barely going to make it."

Bernie and Chas were waiting in the driveway when they reached Grandma's house.

"What took you so long?" Bernie called.

Mom laughed and slammed the car door. "She's not going to make many more trips over those mountains."

What about getting home? What about Mousetrap? Murphy wished they could turn around and head home right away.

A few raindrops splashed on Murphy's face, and the wind snapped in his hair as he stepped out of the car. Three boys who had been kicking a ball behind the truck formed a line on the side of the driveway. They leaned back on their heels and watched Murphy and Mom. The boy that held the ball was Albert; Murphy recognized him from the summer. He had seen the others too, but he didn't know their names.

The boys were bigger than Murphy and older too. They had looks of determination on their faces. Their skin looked tough and leathery, probably from spending a lot of time outside. The day was cold, but their sleeves were short and none wore a jacket.

"Come on in," Mom said to Bernie and Chas.

Grandma opened the front door and said, "Welcome home!"

She threw her arms around Mom, and then she hugged Bernie and Chas.

"Thank you for bringing my kids home," she said.

She reached down and picked up Murphy and swung him around and then around again.

"Good to see you, boy," she said. "You've grown so big I hardly recognize you."

Murphy stumbled when his feet hit the floor. His stomach was woozy from the car ride and now his head spun.

"Hi, Grandma," he said.

His feet steadied on the floor, and he hugged Grandma. She wasn't like Mom. Mom was small. Although Murphy was only nine and almost the shortest boy in his class, Mom was only a bit taller than Murphy when they stood back to back in front of the mirror. When Grandma picked him up, Murphy could feel her thick arms and large hands holding him firm. She was tall and round and when she hugged him he sank into her chest.

Albert and the other boys followed Murphy into the house and leaned against the wall by the door. They watched the newcomers' every move as if they expected something to happen.

"You must be hungry," Grandma said to Mom.

"Yeah," Mom said. "What's for supper?"

"Clam chowder. That's all I had time to cook." Grandma lifted a huge pot from the stove and placed it on a towel that was folded on the table. She set a stack of bowls, a pile of spoons and knives, a plate of fried bread, a pot of jam and a tub of butter next to the soup.

Murphy was starving. For a few minutes, he forgot about Mousetrap and the boys who leaned against the wall. The warm food slid into his stomach and made it stop turning over and over.

"You boys get over here and help yourself," Grandma told Albert and the boys. "These are your relatives, Murphy. Danny stays here with me." She pointed to the shortest of the three boys. But he was still taller and bigger than Murphy. "You already know Albert," Grandma continued. "And Jeff is your Auntie Maggie's son. They live across the field."

The boys shuffled up to the table, forming a line behind Albert. Between mouthfuls, Murphy looked them up and down. He imagined himself making the fourth boy in the line. Up and down he was the shortest by at least a head. Side to side he was only half as wide as any one of them. They had square shoulders like full-grown men, even though Murphy knew they weren't any older than eleven or twelve.

All three boys had thick spiked black hair. Albert's hair was dyed yellow at the tips. Their skin was darker than chocolate. Murphy glanced at the pale skin on the thin fingers that clutched his spoon and then at Albert's hand scooping fried bread from the plate. He peered at his own feet laced neatly into hiking boots, and then caught a glimpse of Albert's feet scuffing across the kitchen floor in enormous running shoes with wet laces dragging behind. They might be relatives, but there wasn't one thing similar about them.

Albert stuffed the soccer ball under his arm and balanced his food with the other as he disappeared into the living room.

"Why don't you go sit with the boys in the other room, Murphy?" Mom asked.

Murphy wagged his head and said, "I'm okay here."

He pushed his chair against the wall and wound his body around his food until he was as small as he could get. He chewed quietly and listened to Mom and Grandma making plans.

"You and Murphy will be fine downstairs," Grandma said. "You can fix it up however you want. The bathroom needs a little work."

"What about the kitchen?" Mom asked.

"You can eat up here with us," Grandma said.

"Mom, you said there would be a kitchen," Mom said. Her voice sounded high and stretched like it did when she came home late from work and she was tired.

"It's not done." Grandma spooned more soup into her bowl. From the sound of her voice the kitchen wasn't a big deal.

"Mom," Mom's voice cracked. "You said."

"We'll get it done," Grandma said. "You'll be fine up here."

Mom put her spoon down and chewed steadily on her bread.

"I'm going downstairs. I want to see what it looks like," she said.

"You'll need to clean up a little," Grandma added as Mom crossed the kitchen and headed down the stairs. Mom didn't wait for Grandma to say any more.

Murphy ate the last spoonful of soup and buttered another piece of fried bread. It was better that Mom looked at the basement apartment alone. He had a feeling it wasn't going to look the way she had described it to him. So he waited until he was completely finished his supper before he got up.

Grandma and Bernie and Chas were talking and the boys were playing video games when Murphy crept through the kitchen and down the stairs.

Creak. Creak.

Each stair made a loud noise. A bare light bulb hung from a wire and cast eerie shadows across the stacks of papers, fishnets, tires, bottles and bags that cluttered the open space in the basement.

"Mom?" he called out.

"Over here, Murphy." Her voice came from a room at the far end of the basement. He hurried through the jumble of stuff and entered a wide-open room. It was empty except for an old chair in one corner and another chair in the middle where Mom sat. A half-built wall next to the window almost hid a toilet and shower.

Mom leaned forward with her elbows resting on her knees and her cheeks pressed firmly into the palms of her hands. Was she crying or just thinking? Murphy walked across the room and sat on the other chair, facing Mom.

She motioned with her hand to Murphy to come toward her. When he got close she pulled him onto her lap and rocked back and forth.

"This is it, Murphy," she whispered. "This is home."

Her warm tears ran down his cheek. Murphy wanted to cry too. It wasn't home.

Where would they put their beds and the sofa and the TV? Would they even use the kitchen table? What about Mousetrap? There were only two small windows, both high up on the wall, but Mousetrap wouldn't have any trouble climbing out if they were open.

5

The rhythm of the windshield wipers lulled Murphy to sleep on the way home. He awoke to bright city lights. Mom's hands gripped the steering wheel, and her eyes were glued to the road.

Finally she asked, "You awake?"

"Yeah," he said. He stretched the fold out of his neck.

"It's going to be okay," she announced.

"Yeah?" Murphy asked. "What's going to be okay?"

"Moving home," Mom said. "To the reserve."

Murphy was still half-asleep, but he didn't think it would be okay.

"Don't you think?" she asked.

He decided to agree with her anyway. "Yeah," he said. "It's going to be okay."

Mom continued. "I remember five things about growing up on the reserve."

She stared at the oncoming car lights and raised one finger off the steering wheel at a time as if to count to five.

"No, six," she said lifting one finger from her other hand. "There are at least six important things that I think you should know right now."

She didn't wait for Murphy to speak.

"Number one," Mom said. "The reserve is usually a place where only First Nations live."

"Yeah," Murphy said. He knew that already. And he knew he was a First Nation, Mom had told him that. They watched movies about First Nations and she read him stories about salmon and potlatches. He went to the museum and watched Uncle Charlie carve totem poles.

"It's important, Murphy, because you don't look like a First Nation. You look more like your father with your blond hair and blue eyes."

"So?"

"Not everyone will think you're a First Nation. They might think you're white—and pick on you. That's what I remember from living there when I was young."

Murphy didn't like how that sounded.

"Number two." Mom continued as if there was nothing left to say about number one. "You will have cousins to play with all the time."

Number two sounded good to Murphy as long as the cousins didn't pick on him.

"Number three. You get to go to the beach all the time. You'll be able to collect stones and shells and arrowheads, all kinds of things."

Murphy said, "I like number three."

"Number four." Mom hesitated for a moment. "Four is that it rains up there. All the time. I remember being muddy and grubby every day. We played outside and there are no side-walks and the roads are gravel."

"So we have to make sure Mousetrap doesn't get outside," Murphy said. "He's not used to getting dirty."

36

"Yeah," Mom said. "That brings me to number five. There are dogs and cats everywhere. Every family has at least three pets not counting the animals that just live on the reserve. They take care of themselves. Not at all like Mousetrap."

Murphy thought of climbing up to the windows to make sure they were closed every time he left the room. Poor Mousetrap, closed up in such a tiny place.

"What's number six?" Murphy asked.

"Number six." Mom's face broke into a huge smile. "Grandma cooks all the time. Not the kind of food you're used to. She cooks duck soup, smoked fish, deer stew, clam chowder, fish eggs, stuff like that. The house always smells like something's cooking. And most of the food comes from the ocean."

Clam chowder didn't taste bad. Salmon and halibut were yummy. But Murphy had seen fish eggs, and he had smelled duck soup and smoked fish. Just the thought of them made the back of his throat stick together.

"I don't like duck soup," he told Mom. "Or smoked fish."

"You'll learn to like it," Mom said without looking his way. "It was the only food we ate when we were kids—along with potatoes, carrots and onions."

Murphy and Mom stared out the window as they turned the corner near the apartment. The six things weren't bad, but Murphy could tell even Mom wasn't excited about all of them.

"There's more than six things," she said. She parked the car and jumped out. "There's a lot more than six things, but that's enough for tonight."

The apartment didn't feel like home when they opened the door. Grandma's basement didn't feel like home either. When Murphy crawled into bed beside Mousetrap he didn't feel like he had a home. That night Murphy dreamed he pulled a drowning cat out of a mucky puddle. The cat shivered and gasped for breath. Murphy wrapped the cat in his jacket and brought him home. He washed the cat with warm water, and as the brown mud swirled down the sink Murphy realized the cat was Mousetrap.

6

The next week flew by. The last weekend in January came too soon. Early Sunday morning Murphy woke up to find Mousetrap standing on the pillow next to his head. Thumps and bangs and groans came from outside his bedroom door. He pulled Mousetrap into his bed and wrapped the sheets over his head.

"I don't want to go," Murphy whispered to his cat.

"Come on, Murphy," Mom called. "Time to get up and out of there."

Bernie opened his bedroom door. "Your mom says your bed is next," she said.

As soon as Murphy got out of bed, Mom folded his sheets, and Chas and Bernie carried his mattress out of the apartment and lifted it into the back of their pickup truck.

Murphy got dressed and walked into the living room. There were stains on the carpet where the sofa had been. Dirty shadows framed where pictures once hung. Murphy didn't like how the apartment felt, dirty and bleak.

Mom called from the front door, "Bring your pajamas and let's go."

"Coming."

He glanced once more in his bedroom. He wouldn't have a bedroom after this. He peered into the bathroom and looked at the bathtub. There was no bathtub at Grandma's either. When he turned and looked into the kitchen he felt Mom's arm on his shoulder.

"We're going to miss this place, aren't we Murphy?" Mom said.

Murphy rubbed the back of his hand against his nose. His eyes stung. He picked up Mousetrap and wrapped his arms around

40

his cat. Mom wrapped her arms around both of them. Murphy could feel Mom's tears, wet on the back of his neck.

"It's going to be okay, Murphy," she said.

The drive to Grandma's took forever even though Mom put on Murphy's favorite tape and they sang at the top of their lungs. Mousetrap sat on Murphy's lap curled in a blanket. He closed his eyes and didn't open them until Mom stopped the car and said, "We're home."

While Bernie and Chas unloaded the pickup, Albert, Jeff and Danny tapped a soccer ball from foot to foot.

"Sure got a lot of stuff," Albert said to Mom as she lugged furniture inside.

"You sure you gonna fit all that stuff in the basement?" Danny asked.

The unloading was almost finished when Mom said, "You boys gonna stand there or help?"

They helped Bernie with the mattresses and then disappeared.

Once the furniture was piled in the middle of the room there was barely space to move.

Murphy uncovered a chair and held on tightly to Mousetrap until Mom said good-bye to her friends and closed the door.

"Leave Mousetrap with me, Murphy," she said. "You go outside and find the boys. I have work to do."

"I'll help," Murphy offered.

"Thanks," she said, "but no. I need to organize."

What help would he be? But what would he do outside with the boys? And what about Mousetrap? What would Mousetrap do without Murphy?

"I said: Go outside," Mom repeated. "You need to play."

Murphy placed Mousetrap on the chair, checked the windows to make sure they were closed and shut the door securely behind him. He sighed with relief. The boys were nowhere in sight. Murphy headed down the sandy path to the beach. Salt air nipped his cheeks. The blustery wind drowned out everything but the sound of waves crashing against the shore. The beach was strewn with gray weather-beaten logs and instead of sand it was covered in small stones of every color. He crouched and sifted the smooth stones through his fingers: green, orange, black, gray, clear white. He even found pink stones the color of Mom's bedspread.

Murphy picked up soft pieces of shell and glass with round edges. There were so many beautiful things. How would he ever decide what to save and what to send back to the beach? First he stuffed a pink stone in his pocket. Next a green stone, then a black stone and a white stone. Soon he realized that every stone looked special, and he began to look at them more closely. He found green stones with orange flecks, pink stones with black veins, motley black and white stones.

He began to separate the stones by color. Pink stones in one line, green stones in the next. At first Murphy was bothered by the rain, but soon he noticed how shiny the stones looked when splashed with raindrops. He rubbed the wet stones between his fingers and watched bright colors emerge.

Murphy heard feet scuffing along the beach. He kept his head down and kept examining the stones. The sound got louder. Soon Murphy could hear at least three, maybe four, sets of feet. When Murphy looked up with a bright pink stone clutched in his hand, Albert plunked his big wet sneaker right in the middle of Murphy's neatly placed lines of stones. Stones flew off the log. Those that remained were shuffled into several multicolored piles.

A lump formed in Murphy's stomach as if he had swallowed armfuls of stones. His arms fell loosely next to his body, which felt limp like a wet dishcloth. His knees grew watery and wobbly.

"You gonna line up all the stones on the beach?" Albert asked.

Murphy's body wouldn't move. Even if he could think of something to say, there would be no sound to his words. His throat had closed up so tight he could barely breathe. Murphy didn't look up. He watched Albert's feet as he kicked the rest of the stones off the log.

"Maybe you're gonna take all the rocks home in your pocket and line them up for your Mommy," Albert's voice cut through

Murphy's stomach, making him have to pee. Bad.

He wished he could look up at Albert and the other boys and say something smart and tough, but his neck bent down deep, and he stared at the beach. He forced himself to stand and lifted his eyes just in time to see Albert fire the soccer ball directly at him. Without thought, Murphy lifted his hands and stopped the ball as it landed hard into his chest. He tried to hold on, but the ball was wet and slippery and fell onto the beach. Pain shot through his lungs and his breathing got mixed up so he had to gasp to get the air down.

"Nice save," Albert said.

7

He wiped his hands across his chest, but it didn't help. The ball had left a dirty splash of mud on the front of his jacket.

What would Mom say?

"You better go home," Albert said. "I can hear your mommy calling you."

Murphy listened for Mom, but all he could hear was the sound of the waves and a humming in his ears. So he wouldn't make matters worse, Murphy ran up the path and straight home hoping to make it in time to pee.

He hurried through the clutter in the basement and into the apartment.

"Have a good time?" Mom asked.

"Yeah, okay," he replied.

"Are you sure everything's all right?"

"Yeah," Murphy said emerging from the makeshift bathroom. "Want some help?"

Mousetrap leaped from behind a stack of boxes into his arms. Murphy buried his chilly hands in Mousetrap's warm silky hair.

"I don't think Mousetrap will like the cats outside," Murphy said. "They look mean and hungry."

"I don't think they're mean," she said. "But we'll keep him in the room."

Murphy wasn't convinced that Mom was really thinking about Mousetrap. She was busy planning and organizing. Murphy thought it would be up to him to make sure Mousetrap was fine.

"Do you like it so far?" Mom asked.

The beds were against the wall near the bathroom. Mom had nailed blankets to the ceiling to make walls to make a little room for Murphy and to separate his bed from hers. It looked like pictures Murphy had seen of Arabian tents.

"I like it," he said. And he did. He pulled the blanket back. It was a little dark around his bed, but it was warm and safe. He put on sheets and his comforter. He covered his pillows and fluffed them up on his bed. Then he found Mousetrap's velvet pillow, overturned a cardboard box and placed his cat's bed on top.

"This is home, Mousetrap," he said.

He unpacked his stone collection and made space for the brightly colored stones he planned on bringing home from the beach. For a moment, it felt like he was home.

Mom and Murphy left together in the morning, Mom to her new job, Murphy to his new school. In the evening, Mom worked at setting things in order. By the end of the week, the room looked almost like an apartment but without a bathtub or a kitchen.

Mom bought a small fridge, a microwave and a hot plate. She set up the kitchen table, and they sat at the table and ate supper just like they used to.

Mom plugged in a lamp beside Murphy's bed so he could read at night. She set up the computer on a table just outside his blanket door. She laid rugs on the floor and squished plants into spots that were barely big enough.

"It looks like home, don't you think?" she said.

After she hung Murphy's kindergarten paintings on the walls and covered the back of the door with the pictures that used to hang on the fridge, he had to agree. It was beginning to look like home.

But it wasn't just like home. Murphy and Mousetrap didn't play hide-and-seek after school. One reason was he didn't have a key for the door; Mom just left it unlocked. The other reason was there weren't many places to hide in the new place. Other than the beds, the toilet and the shower, which were hidden behind blankets, you could see everything in the apartment by standing in one place.

On Saturday morning, Mom and Murphy were eating their cereal when there was a loud knock at the door.

"Who would that be?" Mom said.

When she opened the door, Albert, Danny and Jeff stood in the doorway.

"Murphy here?" Albert said.

"Come in," Mom said.

Murphy slouched in his chair. Who asked them here? Why don't they go away?

"It's good to see you, boys," Mom said. "Murphy hasn't had anyone to play with."

Albert's eyes scanned the room. "Nice place you've set up here."

He rested his leg on the arm of the sofa and said, "I didn't think you'd get all your stuff in here."

He peered at the blanket walls. "You guys' beds in there?"

"Yeah," Mom said.

"Cool," Albert said. "Real cool." First he pulled the blanket back and looked at Mom's bed. Then he looked at Murphy's bed. He motioned with his chin for Danny and Jeff to join him.

"Look at that, eh," he said. "Wow."

Then he turned to Mom. "I'm pretty impressed, Mrs. J. You made this place look like a home."

"Hey, Murphy." Albert turned his attention to Murphy. "You want to come and play soccer with us?"

"Good idea," Mom said. "He's almost finished his breakfast."

Murphy didn't like what he heard. How did Mom know if he wanted to play soccer? He had never played soccer. Whenever his class had played soccer Murphy found some reason why he couldn't. He ignored Albert and concentrated on his spoon.

"Hurry up, Murphy," Mom said. "Don't keep the boys waiting. Find a jacket; it's cold. And don't get your feet too wet."

Murphy finished his cereal slowly, trying to devise a plan to get out of playing with the boys. When he couldn't think of anything he disappeared behind his blanket wall and rummaged through his shelf for a jacket. When he rejoined Mom, Albert stood by the door, soccer ball under one arm and Mousetrap under the other.

"Nice cat," he said. "What's his name?"

"Mousetrap," Mom answered. "Although he's never seen a mouse."

"You should call him Rat-trap. We got rats around here as big as him."

Murphy didn't like Albert holding Mouse-trap, and he didn't like what he heard about rats. He had never seen a rat, but from what he had heard and from what he had seen on TV they were scary animals.

"Have fun, honey. Don't get too cold," Mom said.

He followed the boys out of the basement and down the driveway, keeping a few paces back.

"Don't get too wet, honey," Albert said with a high squeaky voice, mimicking Mom. "Don't get too cold, honey."

Danny and Jeff laughed, and the three of them walked faster. Why did they even ask him to play?

Murphy's question was answered soon enough. "Leave him alone, Albert," Jeff said. "Grandma said we should be nice to him."

"Ever play soccer?" Albert said half turning around.

Murphy didn't want to say no because he knew everyone played soccer on the reserve.

He didn't want to say yes because he knew that as soon as he got on the soccer field they would find out he was lying. So he didn't answer. He dropped his head and watched his running shoes take step after step along the path toward the park.

"You deaf?" Albert hollered. "You got trouble hearing plain English, white boy?"

"Hey, man," Jeff said. "Murphy's my cousin."

"You know how to play soccer?" Albert said.

"Not really," was all Murphy could say.

8

At the soccer field, two boys sat on old wooden bleachers and two others juggled balls from one foot to the other.

"You guys ready?" Albert called.

The boys gathered around him. Albert stood taller than any of the others. One boy was no taller than Murphy. Another boy was light colored with skin not much darker than Murphy's.

"This is Murphy," Albert said. "They say he's a relative. But he ain't no soccer player."

The boys nodded, but no one spoke until Jeff said, "He's my cousin. Murphy just moved here."

Then the small boy called, "Hi," over his shoulder as he ran down the field kicking the ball.

"We're gonna start," Albert shouted.

"Seeing that you haven't played before," Albert said to Murphy, "why don't you play goalie?"

"No way," Jeff said. "You're the goalie, Albert. He's not gonna be able to stop a thing."

"I don't mind," Albert said as if he was doing Murphy a favor. "He can play my position for a while."

A tall kid with big front teeth and glasses laughed out loud. He punched Albert in the side and said, "Let's do it, Al," sounding like they knew something no one else knew.

"I don't think I'd be good as goalie," Murphy said.

No one paid any attention to him. The boys hurried into the field and started passing the ball from foot to foot.

"Just stand here," Jeff said. "And keep the ball out of the net."

The ball flew from player to player so fast Murphy could barely keep his eyes on it. Some boys kicked the ball toward Murphy, and others kicked it the other way. The other goal was empty, which confused Murphy. What sort of game were they playing?

All the kicking took place near the center of the field, so Murphy had time to look at the goal posts behind him. They were far apart. He looked over his head at the bar across the top of the net. It was twice as high as he was. Between the net and where he was standing was a deep puddle of muddy water. If anybody shot the ball at the net there wasn't one chance in a million that Murphy could keep it out.

He watched the boys passing the ball from foot to foot and calling out, "Behind you," "In front," "Over here," "Nice one."

The running looked exhausting, but at that moment Murphy wished he had played soccer at school. At least he would know what they were doing. Being the goalie wasn't turning out so bad as long as the boys kicking the ball away from the net stopped the boys from kicking it toward the net.

All the standing around gave Murphy time to think. What would he do if the ball came hurtling toward him? He needed a plan. It only took him a moment to decide that he would jump out of its way and let it hit the net. After a few shots the boys would learn that Murphy wasn't a goalkeeper. Then maybe they would realize that he wasn't a soccer player either.

Just when Murphy became sure of his plan, he caught a flash of the soccer ball whizzing through the air toward him. Nose level. Straight for his face.

He had no time to think about moving and letting the ball fly into the net. Instead, he raised his hands and stopped the ball just before it smashed into his face. *Splat!* He stumbled backward wet up to his knees in the puddle. He struggled to breathe. His arms and fingers felt like they had been run over by a truck. But the ball was still lodged between them.

He wheezed heavily and stood frozen up to his knees in the mud, still gripping the ball between his hands. Albert charged him, grabbed the ball and yelled, "You're supposed to throw it back in, you idiot!"

Air finally reached Murphy's lungs, and the fuzz in his brain cleared. He heard the boys calling to each other, "Wow, did you see that little white kid make that save?" "He looks like he's been in goal before."

Murphy's joints felt as if they had been welded together. When the play moved away to center field, he tried to loosen up, but before he had time to stretch his neck or even clap his stiff hands together, Albert sprang away from the others and sprinted back toward the net. The ball made a direct line in front of him as if it were tied with a string to the end of his shoe. Before Murphy had time to wonder how Albert kept the ball so close, the ball left Albert's foot like it had been fired from a cannon and zoomed straight toward Murphy's head. Without a thought, he raised his hands to protect his face, only to find the ball once again lodged in his hands.

"Great save, cousin!" Jeff hollered.

Albert grabbed the ball, spitting words through his teeth as he ran away, "You won't be lucky three times, peewee."

It felt like the ball had smashed every bone and strained every muscle that was holding Murphy together. One more hit like the first two and the ball could kill me, thought Murphy. He repeated his plan to himself: When the ball comes toward you, jump out of the way. It was a simple plan, but so far it hadn't worked.

Moments later, the boy with big front teeth and glasses stole the ball, pulled away from the other boys and ran straight toward Murphy. He had plenty of time to line up and shoot the ball into the net far from where Murphy was standing. Murphy would have had no hope of stopping it. Instead, the boy stopped right in front of Murphy, swung his leg back and kicked the ball with the force of a logging truck. The ball spun through the air so fast that Murphy had no time to move.

Murphy raised his hands. He had no other choice. He was paralyzed with fear and his body felt too broken up to get out of the way. For the third time, he caught the ball, but this time it was coming his way so fast that his legs flew up in the air, and his head hit the ground. Black spots turned into total darkness and quiet settled around him except for the sound of bees in his ears. Shiny gold and silver shapes passed in front of his eyes and turned to gray. Soon the shapes turned into boys leaning over him and staring into his face.

Murphy shook his head, and the darkness drew back. He looked at his hands. The ball was still glued between his fingers.

Once the boys saw his eyes open they began slapping each other's hands.

"Wow!"

"What a save!"

"You're great!"

Jeff bent down and pulled the ball out of Murphy's hands. Murphy rolled over and pushed himself into a sitting position. Thick muddy water soaked into his pants and shoes. He staggered, dripping wet, back to the center of the net. His head felt light, as if it was not completely attached to his neck. His hands, arms, fingers, legs and knees felt like they belonged to someone else's body.

And it wasn't over yet. Each time Albert or the boy with big teeth and glasses ran toward the net, they looked Murphy right in the eye and fired the ball directly at him. If they had aimed at the net, they would have got a goal with every shot. That's how Murphy found out they had a plan. Their plan was not to get a goal. It was to hurt him.

Albert took two, three, four, five shots, and each one spun like a meteor right into Murphy. The boy with big front teeth and glasses did the same thing. Each time, Murphy thought about jumping out of the way, but he didn't have enough time so he blocked the ball with his hands. And each time he raised his hands to block the ball, it got stuck between his fingers.

When the game finally came to an end, the boys pounded him on the back. "You're a great goalie!" they said, and, "You must have played soccer before."

Albert grabbed the ball. "You were just lucky, peewee," he said. And the boy with big front teeth and glasses said, "Wait till next game."

Murphy tried to keep up with Albert, Jeff and Danny on the way home, but his legs wouldn't move quickly, and his knees couldn't remember how to bend.

Jeff hung back with him. "You really never played before?" he asked.

"Never," Murphy replied. His voice was thin and squeaky.

"You're a great goalie," he said.

Murphy liked how those words sounded, but he knew there was nothing great about the saves he made. He stopped the ball because he was terrified. He didn't drop the ball because his hands were frozen. And he didn't jump out of the way because he wasn't fast enough. That was the part Jeff didn't understand.

9

When Mom answered the door on Sunday morning Murphy was still in bed.

"He's not feeling so good this morning," she said. "If he's feeling better later I'll get him to catch up with you boys."

Not so good? Murphy was feeling like he had stubbed every part of his body. He felt worse than ever before in his entire life. Ten times worse than the night he threw up five times after eating a rotten hot dog. Twenty times worse than when he had chicken pox all over his body.

He cuddled next to his cat. Mousetrap purred a pleased sort of sound. Mom brought cereal and orange juice to Murphy's bed.

"Ouch," Murphy said as he tried to sit up.

"Do you have a fever?" Mom asked. She sat on the edge of his bed and stroked his forehead.

"No," Murphy said. "I'm not sick."

He told Mom he had played soccer, which was true. He told her that he was a really good goalie, which wasn't so true, but that's what everyone was saying. He also told her that he made a few great saves that knocked him over. She already knew about the puddle because his jacket, pants, shirt, running shoes and even his underwear were covered with mud.

Murphy didn't tell her that Albert and the boy with big front teeth and glasses had hit him on purpose. He didn't tell her that he had blacked out and seen gold and silver stars or how afraid he was when the ball came flying toward him.

On Monday, Murphy could hardly bend his knees to climb the school bus steps. All last week, he had sat near the front on his own, but today one of the boys from the game shoved over and motioned to him to sit near the back with the rest of the players.

"Great goalie," the boy said. "Coming out to the field after school?"

"Maybe," Murphy said, but he meant no.

Some of the boys who had ignored him at school the week before asked him to play on their soccer team at lunch.

"No, thanks," he said and tried to find someplace to hide. No soccer, not now, not for a long time, please.

The only part about soccer that he liked was how everyone wanted to be his friend. Everyone, at least, except Albert and the boy with big teeth and thick glasses. When they walked past Murphy in the hall they bumped him up against the wall or stuck their elbows in his side.

"Wait until the next game," Albert said.

When Murphy got home from school, he opened the apartment door and called, "Come here, Mousetrap."

He checked on and under Mom's bed and his bed. He looked in all the spots his cat could hide. He stood perfectly still. The apartment was silent except for a faint hum of music seeping through the vents from upstairs.

Panic struck Murphy's stomach and crawled up the back of his neck.

His voice got louder. "Mousetrap, come here!"

He lifted the cushions on the sofa and checked the beds again. He looked under the velvet pillow and in the bathroom. He looked in Mom's make-up container and shoebox, places where Mousetrap couldn't possibly fit.

Mousetrap wasn't in the room. Not anywhere.

A freshly folded pile of towels and sheets and a stack of mail lay on the table. Had Mousetrap sneaked out the door while Grandma was leaving things for Mom?

"Mousetrap," Murphy hollered one more time, "please come here."

It was no use. He rushed upstairs.

"Grandma," he called. "Grandma, are you here?"

Danny sat in front of the TV, playing a video game.

"You seen Grandma?" Murphy asked him.

Danny didn't look up. "No," he said.

"Where is she?" Murphy asked.

"How should I know?"

"Have you seen Mousetrap?" Murphy asked again.

"Who's Mousetrap?" Danny asked with his hands stuck to the controls and his eyes glued to the screen.

"My cat, Mousetrap, is missing. Did you see him anywhere?"

"There's a million cats around here," Danny said, still without looking up. "I don't pay attention to any of them."

Murphy turned and ran out the door and down the driveway.

"Mousetrap," he called. A gray cat slept on the front porch and a black cat lay curled up on the hood of a pickup truck parked beside the driveway. He ran toward the bus stop and saw an orange and black and white cat wandering his way and a tabby cat perched on a bench.

"Mousetrap! Mousetrap!" he hollered at the top of his lungs. "Come here, Mousetrap!"

He turned the corner and headed toward a part of the reserve where he had never been before. Rows of houses lined up next to each other.

"You lost?" a boy shouted. It was the boy with the big front teeth and glasses.

"My cat is lost," Murphy answered.

The boy laughed. "You'll never find him around here," he said.

Murphy ran to the end of the road, turned and headed back. His eyes darted under cars, down driveways, onto porches and up stairs. Mousetrap was nowhere to be found. Murphy ran home along the beach and checked between logs and in bushes, but still no Mousetrap.

Murphy trudged back to Grandma's house. "Mousetrap, please, where are you?" he said more and more quietly as he walked along. He checked in all the same places, but it was no use. Mousetrap was lost.

10

Murphy had planned to collect stones from the beach after school. Instead, he crawled into bed and pulled the comforter over his head.

The apartment was dark when Murphy opened his eyes and peeked out from under the covers.

"Murphy," Mom was calling. "Murphy, you here?" she called again.

Murphy didn't answer. Instead, he stumbled out from behind his blanket wall and up the stairs. He blinked his bleary eyes, not believing what he saw.

"Mousetrap?"

out of the towel and gobbled the fish. After supper, Mom combed Mousetrap's hair while he slept so soundly that he didn't even twitch when the comb snagged on a knot.

Mom giggled. "I think he had a rough day," she said.

The next day after school, Murphy opened the apartment door and called, "Mousetrap." He didn't look under the bed or beside the computer. He knew that Mousetrap wasn't hiding. He wasn't home.

A warm pot of soup sat on the table. Did Mom forget to tell Grandma? Did Grandma forget to watch Mousetrap? When was Mom going to get a lock for the door?

Grandma didn't lock her house. People came in and out whether Grandma was home or not. Just like Mom had said, everyone on the reserve is your relation, so people come and go and cats and dogs do too. Now Murphy understood what she meant. No one paid any attention to making sure that cats stayed inside.

No one used keys on the reserve either. Murphy liked that. He could visit Uncle

Charlie's place to play video games anytime he wanted. He didn't even have to knock. And Auntie Jean always made him a peanut-butter-and-jam sandwich when he was there.

He wondered how Mousetrap felt about the reserve, if he was afraid and lost. Murphy grabbed an apple and ran out the door.

"Mousetrap," he hollered. "Where are you?"

Grandma stuck her head out the window. "That cat of yours missing again?" she called out.

"Yeah," Murphy answered. "You seen him?"

"Yeah, I saw him," she said. "I tried to make sure he didn't get out. But as soon as I opened the door to put the soup on the table, he darted between my feet like a shot. He doesn't want to be cooped inside all day."

Before Grandma said anything else, Murphy saw Mousetrap curled up under the car beside the driveway. He was fast asleep next to the orange and black and white cat.

Murphy crouched down and looked under the car. "Come on, Mousetrap. I'm home."

Mousetrap opened his eyes. He looked happy as could be, lying on the dirty, oily ground next to the skinny, orange and black and white cat.

"Mousetrap," Murphy coaxed as he stretched the full length of his arm under the car. "I've got supper for you."

Mousetrap strolled out from under the car and stretched his back. His hair was streaked with black oil from the underside of the car and his paws were gray. Murphy held him away from his body as he packed him into the house.

"Mousetrap got out again today," Murphy told Mom when she got home from work.

"You did?" she said as she stroked Mousetrap's head. His white hair, usually fluffy and soft, hung limp against his body.

"He likes it out there," Murphy said. "He didn't come when I called. He was sleeping under a car next to that ugly orange and black and white cat."

Mom laughed. But Murphy didn't think it was very funny.

"But he's not pure white anymore," Murphy said.

"He doesn't know he's turned a little brown," Mom said.

"He could get lost, or run over, or stolen," Murphy said. "Or the other cats could beat him up."

"He won't get hurt," Mom said. "Cats love it outside. They're like little boys. They like to play with each other."

Not like every little boy. Murphy didn't want to play outside with the boys. He didn't want to get dirty, and he didn't want to get lost or hurt. He wanted to stay inside where it was safe. He wished Mousetrap felt the same way.

11

Each afternoon that week Grandma had some reason to open the door to the apartment, and each day Murphy ran home from the bus and found Mousetrap gone.

Then Grandma would stick her head out the window and call out, "He took off again."

On Friday, Grandma met Murphy before he headed to the basement. "I decided I should let your cat outside," she said. "He likes it outside better."

Mousetrap was happy to see Murphy after school. He was happy to eat salmon or fried halibut. He spent so much time outside that he got a hungry look on his face and gobbled his food like he hadn't eaten for days.

Murphy finally agreed with Grandma. Mousetrap liked playing with the other cats. He liked wandering around the reserve and sleeping under the cars. But he didn't look soft and white anymore. At night, he left dusty smudges on Murphy's sheets when he crawled into bed. Mom said he had to sleep on his velvet pillow because she didn't want to wash Murphy's bedding every day.

At least Mousetrap gave Murphy a way to avoid playing soccer with the boys. Tuesday afternoon on the bus, Jeff had said, "Hey Murphy, want to play soccer at the field?"

"Gotta go straight home and find my cat," Murphy answered.

Wednesday, Jeff asked the same question, "You coming to play soccer?"

"I'm not feeling so good yet," Murphy said.

Thursday, Jeff said, "Come on cousin, we miss you in goal."

"Maybe later. My mom wants me to clean up the apartment." Murphy felt bad when he told Jeff a lie. So on Friday he got on the bus late and sat in the front behind the driver to avoid Jeff's invitation. When the bus stopped at the end of their street he hurried off and ran home without stopping.

Murphy felt relieved. Maybe now the boys would forget about him. Maybe he wouldn't have to play soccer again, ever, in his whole life.

"Time to get up," Mom called to Murphy with a cheery voice. It was Saturday and Murphy had the whole day to himself. He lay still for a few minutes thinking that he would take some containers to the beach and collect stones. Thin rays of sun filtered through the window. It was warm—a perfect day for the beach. Maybe Mom would come too.

"Hey, you," Mom said as she pulled back the bedroom curtain, "I'm going into town with Auntie Brenda this morning."

"I wanted to go to the beach," Murphy said. "And I wanted you to come too. There's real colorful stones there."

"Maybe tomorrow," Mom said. "I've already made plans."

"I'll come with you then," Murphy said.

"You won't want to shop with the women," she said. "I won't be gone long."

Before Mom finished talking there was a loud knock on the door. Murphy rolled over and faced the wall. He pulled his blankets over his head, but he could still hear Albert's voice: "Hey. Murphy here?"

Not again.

"Yeah," Mom said. "He's still in bed." Then she called out, "Murphy, the boys are here."

Murphy didn't move.

"We're playing soccer," Jeff said. "Murphy was goalie last weekend. Did he tell you?"

"Kind of," Mom said.

"Yeah," Albert said. "We'll see how good he is this weekend."

He lay still, but Mom persisted.

"Come on, Murphy, the boys are waiting."

Murphy felt like someone had pushed him into a corner and was leaning on him. There was nothing he could do. He couldn't say he was going shopping with Mom; she'd just said no to that. He couldn't say he didn't feel well; Mom knew better.

"Hurry up, Murphy!" Jeff called out. "We'll wait upstairs."

"Don't keep us waiting too long," Albert added. Then the door shut.

"I'm so glad the boys like playing with you," Mom said. "Cousins everywhere just like I said."

She didn't know anything. She couldn't tell from the sound of Albert's voice that Murphy would be lucky to get home alive.

He got up, changed and ate a bowl of cereal without saying much. Mousetrap sat next to him. Murphy stroked Mousetrap's head and looked at how his cat had changed in just a couple of weeks. He looked tougher, leaner, but happy enough. Mom looked happy too. Shopping trips with her cousin, more money at work, Grandma upstairs, her sisters close by—the reserve was a good place for Mom. And it was a good place for Mousetrap. But it didn't feel like a good place for Murphy.

"I'm heading out now, Murphy," Mom said. "You have a good time."

"Yeah, sure," Murphy said.

"I'll be home to make supper," Mom added.

"Yeah, sure."

After Mom left, Murphy slipped on his old jacket and headed out the door.

"Stay inside today, Mousetrap," he said. "You never know what could happen to you out there."

Murphy crept up the stairs and walked into Grandma's kitchen. Albert was lounging on a kitchen chair. "It's about time," he said. "What were you doing? Curling your hair?"

Danny had joined Jeff and Albert, and together the four boys headed for the field.

"Hey, Albert," the boy with big front teeth and glasses called out when he joined them.

"Hey, Levi," Albert gave him a high five. "It's gonna be a good game today."

Two boys were waiting at the field when Murphy and the others arrived. They were tall and looked even older than Albert.

"You the guy that can play goalie?" one of them asked.

Murphy ignored his question. He didn't want to say that there had been a big mistake—he wasn't really a goalie at all.

"This the guy?" the other boy asked Albert. "We heard he's really got hands. Snags the ball and doesn't let go."

"Whatever," Albert sneered. "We'll see how good he is."

Two more boys appeared.

"Haywire, Rory," Jeff shouted. "What's going on?"

Haywire wasn't much taller than Murphy. After a moment, Murphy decided he wasn't much older either. Rory had light brown hair and skin—almost as light as Murphy. And he was only eight or nine years old.

Murphy stepped away from the circle the boys had formed around Albert and Levi. They slapped each other on the back and made plans to form a team for a tournament.

"Yay, Buckskins!" Albert shouted. "We'll do it this year!"

"We're number one!" Levi hollered.

All the boys clapped and cheered.

Murphy thought of making a getaway for home. He wasn't part of a team. No one would notice if he was missing. The boys were too big and loud. They knew how to play soccer. They were number one. Buckskins didn't sound like Murphy's kind of team whatsoever.

12

"Where were you guys?" Levi asked when four more boys joined the group.

"Getting here," said a tall boy with long hair. "We wanna see the new kid play goalie."

"Yeah, we hear he's really good," another boy added.

Jeff motioned toward Murphy with his chin. "That's him," he said. "He's my cousin."

"That white kid?" the long-haired boy asked. "He's your cousin?"

Blood rushed into Murphy's cheeks. His throat felt like a dry sponge. He choked down his breath. Kids on the school bus called him white kid and white boy and whitey. He had been called other names as well, like honky, which he thought might have something to do with being white. The words were usually said in a way that made Murphy feel bad inside. No one had said anything about him being white when he lived in the city. But there were people of all colors there. Here he stuck out like a red banana.

"Yeah, he's Auntie Lisa's son," Jeff said. "You got a problem with that?"

"Hey, man," the boy said, raising his hands up. "No problem."

"Just doesn't look like a goalie to me," the other boy added.

"We'll see how white he is after he rolls around in the puddle a few times," Albert said.

Murphy turned his back on the boys. Why did he get out bed? Why didn't he go to town with Mom and Auntie Brenda?

"You're in the goal," Jeff said. "Keep your eye on the ball, cousin."

Most of the boys ran to center field. Murphy trudged toward the net.

"I'm defense," Jeff called to Murphy. "Those guys are offense."

He motioned with his hand, but Murphy couldn't tell who was who. From the way they walked toward center field, hitting each other's backs and laughing, he knew that Albert and Levi were going to shoot at him.

Did they have the same plan as the last game—to kill him?

Murphy's stomach churned as he thought of standing in the net while the ball smashed into his body. Still, he felt proud when Jeff called out, "Way to go, Murphy! Let's see some great saves."

"Way to go, keeper," Rory called out.

The boy with long hair and long legs added, "Let's see you do it." Murphy had heard the boys call him Junior.

While the boys ran from one side of center field to the other, passing and kicking the ball from foot to foot, Murphy made a plan:

GET OUT OF THE WAY OF THE BALL;

DON'T EVER GET IN FRONT OF THE BALL;

DON'T LIFT YOUR HANDS AND CATCH THE BALL.

It was a simple plan. If it worked, the boys would pull Murphy out of the net, and he could go to the beach and collect stones. The best part of the plan was that he wouldn't get hurt. Not one bit. The ball would whiz by his body and smash into the net. Murphy repeated his plan over and over again.

Murphy thought about the plan as Levi broke away from the other players with the ball. Jeff scrambled to get the ball back, but Levi tapped it to the left and neatly side-stepped around Jeff's body. That left Levi rushing in a straight line toward Murphy.

He braced himself. His plan was in place: GET OUT OF THE WAY OF THE BALL. But before he had time to move a muscle, the ball was hurtling through the air at his face. Instinct took over. Murphy's arms flew up. *Splat*! The wet ball shot mud in his eyes, nose and mouth as it lodged itself in Murphy's hands. Murphy stumbled back a few steps blinded by the force of the shot and the mud.

Instead of falling into the puddle and rolling around in pain, like he did last game,

Murphy stayed on his feet. And instead of standing paralyzed with the ball frozen in his hands, Murphy wiped his eyes with the back of his sleeve and tossed the ball to Jeff.

As the boys ran back to center field, he heard Haywire yelling, "Great save, keeper."

"The white boy can catch," Junior shouted.

Before Murphy had time to enjoy what the boys were saying, Levi had a second break-away. GET OUT OF THE WAY OF THE BALL, Murphy thought fiercely. This time Levi's shot was faster and harder. Once again the instinct to protect himself overtook Murphy's plan. His body froze, but his arms flew in front of the ball.

The ball hit with the force of a freight train, but Murphy's feet remained glued to the ground. He barely took the time to wipe his eyes or feel the pain before he stepped forward and tossed the ball toward Jeff. The only boys who weren't cheering for him were Levi and Albert. They lingered close by so that Murphy could hear Albert say, "Next time you won't have a chance."

Although Levi's shots were harder than ever, all Murphy could feel was a dull numbness as if his blood had stopped flowing. He clapped his hands together and rubbed his knees. He bent up and down. Maybe he needed to limber up so that he could jump out of the way of the ball. He pulled on his ankles the way he had seen the other boys stretch their legs. Then he jumped from side to side.

When Murphy raised his eyes a crowd of players had appeared near center field. Jeff was nowhere to be seen, and Albert was zipping down the field toward the net. His eyes were fixed on Murphy's face as the ball whizzed in a straight line near his toe. Murphy locked his eyes onto Albert's. He felt fear. His body was supple. This time he would get out of the way.

Out of the corner of his eye, Murphy saw Albert shift his body and drive the ball toward Murphy's right side. At the same time Murphy's body was moving. His arms and legs and hips and shoulders sprawled toward the right. Instead of getting out of the way, he was positioning himself right in front of the ball.

Splat!

Just like before, the ball blasted into his chest. He stumbled backward a few steps, hands glued on the ball, until he was up to his ankles in the puddle. He steadied himself, stepped out of the water and threw the ball toward center field.

Murphy's eyes locked with Albert's again. Albert's plan to hurt Murphy hadn't worked. His plan to show the boys that Murphy was no goalie also hadn't worked. Murphy's plans hadn't worked either. At first, when Albert and Levi shot right at his body, he hadn't moved one bit. Then when Albert drove the ball past his body toward the net, he moved in front of the ball. His body and his mind were not cooperating.

The boys erupted in a chorus of praise.

"Wow!" "Wow, white boy!" "Wow!" Their voices where loud. Even the boys on offense ran toward the goal and raised a high five to Murphy.

Rory leaped into the air and wrapped his

legs around Murphy. "Way to go! I've never seen a save like that!" he said as he jumped down.

Each boy on his side filed past and gave him a two-handed hug. Everyone was excited about the save except for Albert and Levi, who turned and walked back up the field with their heads bent toward the ground. They didn't say one word to each other. At least none that Murphy could hear.

Murphy shook his body like a wet dog. He stretched each leg and then his shoulders. He pulled his fingers and arms and jumped with both feet into the air. As he jumped he moved his neck from side to side. He was making moves. Yes. They felt good. Murphy had seen soccer players on TV and at school limbering up, getting ready, and he looked just like them. He knew it. After a few moments most of the pain disappeared.

That's when Murphy changed his plan.

"Get in front of the ball," Murphy said to no one but himself. "Don't jump out of the way. Jump into the way. Then shake it off."

From then on Murphy practiced his new plan. He concentrated on the players' bodies as they neared his goal. He studied the way they shifted from side to side. When the shooter was close enough he looked up and stared directly into his eyes. Only out of the corner of his eye did he see the player's foot connect with the ball. But each time he saw enough to know exactly which way the player would aim. When the ball left the striker's foot, Murphy's body shot in front of it, almost without thought, and fast enough to stop it from going into the net.

It worked almost every time. Only two shots got past Murphy that afternoon. Both goals were scored by a boy they called Big Foot. He had a way of dribbling the ball until he was so close that Murphy couldn't see which way Big Foot was going to shoot. Then he drove the ball at such a sharp angle Murphy's body didn't have a chance to move one way or the other.

Although Albert's shots got more and more forceful, Murphy had no trouble blocking them. It was Levi's strikes that hurt the most. Levi didn't try to get a goal. He just shot the ball right at Murphy. Each time Levi kicked the ball, it sped faster than the time before. Once it hit Murphy so hard in the chest that it knocked the breath right out of his lungs. Black spots blocked his sight as he bent down and opened his mouth to pull air into his windpipe. Luckily, before he fell over, he finally swallowed a lump of air. It killed his throat, but at least he didn't pass out.

"Way to go!" Jeff said when the game was over. "You're great. I thought you said you never played before."

"Yeah, man," Haywire said. "Looks like we got our keeper for the tournament."

Even Big Foot, who played for the other side, grabbed Murphy and tossed him into the air. "Great goalie," he said. "For such a little white guy."

"Don't worry about him, cousin," Jeff said. "He doesn't mean anything by it."

Being called little white guy didn't sound so bad, not this time.

"Why doesn't he just go home where he belongs?" Albert sneered.

"This is his home," Jeff replied. "And you're an awesome forward. So why don't you just let him be our goalie?"

On the way home, the boys talked about the Easter weekend tournament.

"Six weeks are all we got," one of the big boys said. "Dad said he's registered our team. He'll be here tomorrow."

"I heard there's gonna be ten teams or more," Haywire said.

When Murphy heard that the tournament was going to be held in the city, not far from his old apartment, he was excited. Mom would be excited too.

"You gotta be out tomorrow," Jeff said as Murphy headed down Grandma's driveway. "Uncle Rudy'll want to see you. He'll pick you for sure to be the keeper."

"See ya tomorrow," Murphy called out. He was beginning to like living on the reserve.

He reached under the car and pulled Mousetrap up into his arms. Mousetrap was gray, and his feet were sandy and dirty. Murphy looked at his own hands. They were covered in thick mud, and spots of dirt were splattered up his sleeves and all across his jacket. His legs were soaking wet, and his feet sloshed in his running shoes.

Mom opened the door and stared at the grubby twosome. "Oh, my," she said, laughing, "it looks like you two have had fun."

Murphy pulled off his shoes, and water sploshed across the floor. He changed his wet clothes, wiped up the mess and curled on the sofa next to Mom and Mousetrap. He told them about the game and about Albert and Levi's plan to hurt him.

"I had a plan too," he explained. "GET OUT OF THE WAY OF THE BALL."

"Why?" Mom asked.

"Because then the boys would figure out I wasn't a goalie, and they would pull me out of the game."

"That's not a good plan," Mom said.

"It didn't work anyway," Murphy said. "When they kicked the ball at me I couldn't move. I was too scared. And once I had loosened up I moved right in front of the shots."

"Wow," Mom said. "So it worked out in the end."

"I guess so," he said. "I still can't really believe it. They all think I'm a goalie."

Murphy was so proud that tears spurted down his still-grubby cheeks. "I saved Albert's shot, Mom. And then I saved the next one and the next one."

Mom listened quietly while Murphy explained. Even Mousetrap was interested in his story.

"I only missed two shots. Big Foot kicked them both. He was up so close I didn't have a chance," Murphy said. "I'll figure it out. And get them next time."

13

Uncle Rudy was waiting at the field when Murphy and Jeff arrived the next day.

"I'm going to sit right here and watch," he said as the boys gathered around the bleachers. "I want you boys to play just like you do every day. Ignore me. Pretend I'm not here."

"Hey, Uncle," Albert said as he sauntered toward the bleachers. Did that mean Albert was Murphy's cousin? Couldn't be, Murphy thought. But then, like Mom said, all the kids were cousins.

"You playing shooter or keeper, nephew?" Uncle Rudy asked.

"Shooter," Albert said. "We got a new keeper."

"Really?" Uncle Rudy looked surprised. "Who?"

"Murphy," Albert replied. Murphy stared at him. He almost sounded as if he was happy to be replaced in the net.

"And he's good too. Right, cousin?" Jeff added, slapping Albert on his back.

Had Jeff talked to Albert?

"You mean Lisa's boy?" Uncle Rudy looked right past Murphy. "They moved home. That's right."

Jeff pointed his nose toward Murphy. "That's him right there," he said.

"Welcome home, boy," said Uncle Rudy. He smiled so big he showed a mouthful of white teeth. "I'm glad my little cousin finally moved home. I've missed her. You tell her cousin Rudy can't wait to tease her again."

He roared with laughter as if he remembered something that no one else knew about.

"Okay, enough of that," he said, clearing his throat. "I'm on the bench. You boys play your game. Like I said, forget I'm here."

It wasn't hard for Murphy to forget that Uncle Rudy was there. Balls flew at him from every angle. The boys were trying extra hard to impress the coach. Each time the ball came toward him, Murphy found a way to get in front of it. Even Big Foot couldn't get the ball past Murphy. Only two goals were scored, and this time Albert kicked both of them. When he let the second shot fly, Murphy leaped toward the right side of the net as if he had springs in his feet. For a split second his body was airborne. The ball stung the tips of Murphy's fingers as it flew into the net, and his body dropped like a dead weight onto the muddy field.

Even though the ball got by, Murphy knew that it was the best move he had ever made in the net.

"Great goal," Uncle Rudy hollered at Albert. Then he shouted, "That's some goalie we have. You gotta be good to get a shot past him."

Albert seemed to like what he heard. Murphy did too.

In the following weeks, the boys practiced every day after school. When the school bus dropped Murphy off at the corner, he ran home and checked under the cars until he found Mousetrap.

Then he stretched his arm until he could pull the cat toward him. "Get over here," he said. "I got a quick treat for you, and then I have to get to the field."

Each day he scooped canned salmon into a bowl and waited impatiently until Mousetrap gobbled his treat. Then Mousetrap rejoined the other cats under the car, and Murphy rushed over to the field.

On March 23, the Wednesday before the Easter tournament, Uncle Rudy brought a paper to practice.

"We're all signed up," he said. "Here's the schedule for our first two games. And here's the roster."

Murphy peered over Uncle Rudy's shoulder and scanned the roster. Beside GOALIE Uncle Rudy had written, MURPHY JONES.

"Who's our spare goalie?" Uncle Rudy asked the boys.

The boys looked from one to the other, most eyes stopping at Albert.

"You?" Uncle Rudy said. "You the only spare goalie we got?"

"I guess," Albert said. He didn't look very enthusiastic.

"We can't lose you on the offense. We need your goal scoring ability," Uncle Rudy said. One by one he eyed the boys. "Doesn't anyone else play goalie? What about you, Jeff?"

Jeff laughed. "No way," he said. "You don't want me in the goal."

"What about you, Levi?"

"No chance. They don't call me Vacuum Cleaner for nothing."

Each boy shook his head. "Not me." "Not me." "I'm hopeless." "I'm worse than that." There were only two goalies on the team, Murphy and Albert.

"That means you better not get sick, Murphy," Uncle Rudy said, "or hurt." He placed his hand on Murphy's shoulder. "We're counting on you."

When the boys walked home, Albert caught up to Murphy. "You gotta be there," he said. "We're gonna win this tournament."

"I'll be there," Murphy said. "Don't worry."

"You're really good," Albert said. He spoke quietly. He wasn't used to saying nice stuff to people, thought Murphy, and he didn't want the other boys hearing his words. "I'm glad I gave you my position, cousin."

"Me too," Murphy said.

Thursday night, everyone packed their cars with tents, clothes and soccer gear and drove south on the road out of the village. Grandma, Danny, Uncle Charlie and Auntie Jean and lots of others.

Murphy remembered watching soccer at the Easter tournament since forever. First Nations teams of boys, men, women and girls competed for trophies and prizes. People from villages all over the province gathered to cheer on their players.

This year Murphy wasn't just a spectator. He was a player. Mom, Grandma, Chas and Bernie would spread their blankets on the grass and sip from their thermoses as they watched him.

"Put out three bowls of food," Mom said to Murphy. "One for each day we'll be gone."

Murphy asked, "What if he eats them all at once?"

"He'll have a stomach ache, and he'll be hungry for a few days," Mom said. "It won't hurt him."

"But..."

"He'll be okay," Mom said. "We'll leave the window open so he can climb in and out if he wants."

Mousetrap's ears perked up as he watched Murphy fill three bowls. He nosed the food, then wandered behind Murphy and Mom as they packed the last few things into the car.

In just two short months everything had changed. Mousetrap was perfectly contented being left behind. Mom was happy to leave him. And although Murphy didn't want to admit it, deep inside he knew his cat would be fine without him.

"Bernie and Chas are so excited," Mom said. "They have a bed for you, and I'm going to sleep on the couch. They can't wait to watch you play."

14

Friday morning, they arrived at the park at nine thirty, sharp. Soccer games were in progress on all three fields.

"We have half an hour," Mom said and pointed across the park. "There's your team."

Uncle Rudy and a few boys were huddled on the sidelines. Mom, Murphy, Chas and Bernie found a good spot to watch the game. They spread a blanket on the field and plopped their bags and bodies on top.

"Go on, Murphy," Mom said.

"Good luck," Chas called out.

"Give us gold," Bernie hollered.

Murphy walked through the crowd to his team. The boys were yanking new red team shirts over their heads. When he saw Murphy, Uncle Rudy reached into the duffel bag and pulled out a black shirt splashed with red, green and purple. There was a bright gold star on the front instead of *Buckskin Bulldogs* like the other boys' shirts.

"Here," he said. He held the shirt up for all the boys to see. "Look at the keeper shirt."

When he turned it around Murphy saw *KEEPER* printed boldly from shoulder to shoulder. Underneath was a large number one. The other boys stood back and admired the brightly colored shirt. The team shirts looked great, but Murphy was extra proud to wear his keeper shirt as he walked toward the net.

He stretched and pulled his arms and legs. He lifted his chin and turned his head from side to side. He squatted and jumped. His stomach still had a heavy lump that turned over and over. His body felt stiff as cardboard, and his brain felt soft as mush. He kept his eyes on Jeff and his other team members. He tried to close his ears to the spectators, but it was pretty hard to block out the sound of parents shouting, "Go Buckskins," and, "Go Shooters." It sounded like a thousand people were cheering for the other team.

Once the whistle blew and the action started, Murphy stood in his net and waited. The other team might have been called the Shooters, but they didn't send very many shots his way. By the end of the game he had only touched the ball six times. Albert and Big Foot got three goals each and Junior and even Haywire got one each. The score was eight to zero for the Buckskin Bulldogs.

"Three o'clock this afternoon," Uncle Rudy said. "Don't be late. Our next game starts at three thirty. It's all or nothing from now on. We lose, we're out of the tournament. We win, we're in the final game."

In the afternoon the park was packed. This time when Murphy readied himself in the net, he watched the crowd and waved at Mom, Chas and Bernie.

"Hey, Grandma," he called out.

"Show me what you can do, grandson," she shouted.

When the whistle blew Murphy tried to concentrate on the players, but his eyes wandered around the field. The spectators were so noisy that he couldn't hear his own team members or Uncle Rudy. A jumble of players moved down the field toward him. Murphy strained his eyes to find the ball. It was hidden in a confusion of legs and feet until out of nowhere it whizzed directly toward the net. In an instant of pure instinct, Murphy's body sprang right in front of the ball. The crowd erupted as he lay on the ground still wondering what happened.

Lucky. How did he do it?

"Way to go, Murphy," Mom, Chas and Bernie hollered as he pulled himself off the ground.

Out of the scramble of voices Uncle Rudy's voice was clear, "Great save, Murphy Jones."

A few seconds later a crowd of players jostled only a few body lengths in front of the net. Murphy dodged from side to side, trying to anticipate where the ball would come loose. There was no telling where he should stand. When the ball finally shot free from the legs and arms, Jeff wound up and kicked it back to center field.

The score at the end of the second game was two to zero. Albert and Big Foot picked up Murphy and held him over their heads as they ran to the sidelines. They tossed him into the crush of team members.

"Way to go, Murphy!"

"You're great!"

"Another shutout!"

"The best keeper!"

Murphy's ears rang. The cheers smashed into his head. He was glad enough that they won. It wasn't that. It was that he didn't feel like the best keeper. He didn't feel like a keeper at all. He felt lucky. From the bottom of his stomach, he could feel he was a fake. He wasn't a keeper at all—it was a lie.

Buckskin Bulldog fans crowded around the team.

"Way to go, team," Mom, Chas and Bernie hollered as they slapped the boys on their backs.

"We did it, boys," Uncle Rudy announced. "We're in the final game tomorrow afternoon—two o'clock, sharp. Be here. The game starts at two thirty."

"You're playing the Island Thunderbirds," Mom said as they climbed in the car. "They've won their games ten to two and twelve to four. They're the team to beat, Murphy."

"Exciting stuff," Bernie said. "Can't wait for tomorrow."

Murphy could wait. He wished tomorrow would never come. The feeling in his belly made him wish he could wrap himself in bed with his cat and not poke his head out from under the covers for a week.

By two thirty Saturday afternoon the sun had disappeared behind a thick mass of dark gray clouds. Spits of rain fell on the spectators huddled under blankets and umbrellas. The players bobbed up and down, rubbing their arms and legs to keep warm.

"Okay, boys," Uncle Rudy said. "It's been a long day waiting for our game. Stay warm."

Murphy pulled a blanket tightly around his shoulders. While the boys called to one another, "We're gonna win!" and, "Look at that trophy!" all Murphy could think was, I wish I wasn't here. They're all going to find out that I'm a big fake.

The previous game ended at two twenty. As the last player walked toward the sidelines, another team ran toward center field. They were big. Bigger than Big Foot. They looked like teenagers, but they couldn't be older than twelve—that was the rule. They wore black-and-white striped uniforms. They looked like the referee except for the red bandanas they had tied on their heads. The bandanas made Murphy think more of gangsters than soccer players.

Murphy dropped his blanket and ran toward the net. His body was instantly covered with goose bumps. He was afraid and he was cold. If only he didn't have to be there.

Jeff kicked the ball in Murphy's direction. "Here," he called out. "Come on, cousin, get in the game."

At first Jeff kicked the ball softly. Murphy picked it up and tossed it back. Jeff kicked it harder and harder until he was driving the ball toward the net. Murphy dodged left and then right, never once missing Jeff's shots.

"That's better," Jeff said. "You got it, Murphy. Don't forget."

Murphy was still warming up when Jeff turned toward center field and the game began. His eyes searched frantically for the ball as a boy came striding toward him. The ball spun halfway between the player and Murphy. Murphy's body froze. From his head to his toes he was a block of ice. Cold and useless. The player turned his foot and drove the ball up and over Murphy's head into the net.

Murphy didn't move until Albert shouted, "Get the ball!"

The opposing team erupted into cheers and jaunted to center field. The Buckskins remained quiet. They slumped their shoulders and dragged their feet back to their positions. No one said a thing. Not Uncle Rudy. Not even Jeff.

The only thing Murphy heard was Mom's thin shrill voice, "Don't worry. You'll get the next one."

His body was stiff, and his brain was dead. They weren't working together. They weren't working at all. It was a mumbo jumbo of confusion. He couldn't hear his own thoughts because of the spectator noise. He couldn't see the ball because his eyes stung from the rain and wind and salty tears that pooled under his eyelids. Mom, Chas and Bernie, and Uncle Rudy had disappeared in the crowd. The only thing Murphy could hear, see or feel was a numb roar coming from inside his body.

Just as he thought he was going to keel over and pass out Jeff ran back toward the net.

"Murphy! Murphy!" he shouted. "Come on, get with the game!"

Murphy heard his cousin but stood motionless.

"Shake it off, cousin," Jeff shouted.

As if plugs fell out of Murphy's ears he heard Uncle Rudy hollering, "We'll get it back! On your toes, Murphy!"

Murphy shook his body from head to toe. He began to feel his blood flowing through his veins as the crowd of players moved quickly past center field toward him. His eyes darted between the feet to find the ball. The Thunderbirds passed from one player to the next with such speed Murphy's eyes could hardly follow the play.

For a few moments before the half time whistle blew, the players' backs turned to Murphy while they charged at the Thunderbird net. Murphy didn't see what happened, but moments later Albert dashed back to center field, waving his arms in the air.

"Got one!" Uncle Rudy roared.

Mom and Chas and Bernie shot into the air, slapping hands and hugging each other as if the game had been won.

The whistle blew. The score was one–one.

The team formed a circle and shouted, "Way to go! Look out, Thunderbirds! We're coming back!"

Murphy didn't think so, and it seemed that Uncle Rudy didn't either. "They've outplayed us the whole game," he said. "We won't win that way. One shot wonders—that's not us."

The boys gulped water from bottles. They grew quiet.

"Levi, where are you? Albert, wake up! We don't call you Big Foot for nothing, where is it?" Uncle Rudy's voice was loud. He cuffed the boys on the shoulders. "Haywire, Jeff, you guys gotta be there. Murphy, stay awake out there. We need shots. Good shots. Murphy's not getting much help out there."

When the second half began, the Thunderbirds continued to dominate the play. One shot after the other flew at Murphy. After the first couple his body and his mind woke up. He watched the play; he watched the players; he kept his eye on the shooter's eye. When a foot kicked the ball, out of the corner of his eye he could see exactly where it was headed, and instinct sent his body in the right direction.

But like Uncle Rudy had said, Murphy wasn't getting much help from the other players. The Thunderbirds were slick. The ball moved from one player to the other like it was set to music. Albert, Levi and Big Foot scrambled to take it, but they ended up turning circles and bumping into each other. Levi tumbled onto his butt, and a Thunderbird

115

offense leaped over his body and flew past Jeff and Haywire like they were standing still. Murphy was almost dizzy by the time the player wound up to take a shot. Without hesitation, Murphy's body flew out to meet the ball. But instead of the ball lodging itself in his hands, the greasy leather spun around in his arms and spurted out. Before Murphy had time to retrieve it, the ball rolled past the goal line and rested up against the net.

Slowly Murphy walked back and picked up the slippery ball. The team was a shambles. And Murphy losing the ball didn't help. The score was two to one for the Thunderbirds.

"We got time," Uncle Rudy shouted. "We got time!"

Not much time. The game was almost over, and nothing but a fluke could bring the Buckskins a win.

From the sidelines a chorus erupted, "Buckskins! Buckskins! Buckskins!" Mom and Chas and Bernie had been joined by other moms and dads and fans from home. They held their hands in the air, swayed from side to side and called each player by name, "Big Foot! Albert! Jeff! Haywire! Levi! Danny!" Grandma was there and Auntie Jean and Uncle Ray; everyone from home shouted together, "Reggie! Frankie! Murphy! Junior!"

Murphy gulped down a lump in his throat and squished back tears.

"Come on!" he shouted.

Then Jeff shouted and Albert and Big Foot. Haywire and Reggie called to each other, "We can do it!"

With any luck, Murphy thought, we will. Only a few minutes later he saw the backs of his players again. Again Albert rushed back to center field, this time carrying Haywire on his shoulders.

"Haywire! Haywire! Haywire!" the crowd yelled.

The score at the end of the game was two–two.

15

Now what? Murphy had never been in a tie game. Did they both win the trophy?

He ran to the sidelines.

"Penalty shots," Uncle Rudy said. "Five each side. Whoever gets the most goals wins."

The boys turned and looked at Murphy.

"What are penalty shots?" Murphy asked.

Uncle Rudy explained while the other boys stood quietly.

"You are in the net. They send out their best shooters. The shooter stands at the penalty line until the referee blows the whistle. Then the shooter takes his best shot. Him against you. Then it's our turn. Our shooter against their keeper." Uncle Rudy held his hand on

Murphy's shoulder. "You have never been in goal for penalty shots?"

"Never."

It was a good thing Murphy didn't know about penalty shots or he would have wanted to run home before they started. Uncle Rudy was right. They picked their best shooters and their biggest shooters. The first shot rocketed into Murphy's chest almost driving him back into the net.

After one shooter from each side had taken a turn, the score for penalty shots was zero–zero.

The next two shooters for the Thunderbirds missed the net entirely. So did Levi and Danny.

After three shooters from each side had gone, the score for penalty shots was still zero–zero.

The next shooter for the Thunderbirds made Murphy's knees shake. He was the biggest of all. Murphy tried to look into the boy's eyes, but they were thin slits. As the boy fired the ball, he opened his mouth and let out a scream that sent chills through

Murphy's body. Murphy flew through the air and landed in the far-left corner of the net. The ball was nowhere to be seen. It wasn't until he stood up that Murphy saw the ball in the opposite corner up against the goal post. One goal for the Thunderbirds.

Big Foot steadied the ball on the penalty line. He stepped back and aligned a shot but stopped before he moved his foot. He walked slowly toward the ball a second time and turned the ball over and over slowly until he had it just right. He backed up again and pulled his leg back, connecting with the ball with such force that he sent it shooting past the goalie like a cannonball.

After four shooters from each side the score for penalty shots was one–one.

The last Thunderbird shooter set the ball on the line. He eyed the ball. He eyed Murphy. He drew his eyes from one side of the net to the other. Then he looked directly into Murphy's face. Murphy could feel the boy's piercing look. Murphy didn't move. He kept his gaze on the boy. When the shooter wound up to kick, out of the corner of Murphy's eye he saw the boy turn slightly as he drove the ball. Without a thought Murphy's body met the ball in midair. He curled his thighs and shoulders around the slippery leather and landed in a heap on top of the ball.

Every Buckskin player rushed to meet him.

He did it. He did all he could do. Now it was all up to Albert.

Albert set the ball on the line. The crowd hushed. Although there were hundreds of adults, kids and even babies around the field, it was quiet except for the rush of cars on the street below.

The Thunderbird goalie quivered. He slapped his hands and tugged on his gloves. Murphy thought, Why didn't I use gloves?

Albert took his place. Murphy held both hands on his stomach to hold his guts inside. Albert stepped toward the ball and tapped it with the side of his toe. As if in slow motion the ball spiraled around and around past the feet of the goalie, who barely moved, and into the bottom left corner of the net.

After all ten shooters, the score for penalty shots was two to one, Buckskin Bulldogs over the Island Thunderbirds.

In the picture Albert holds the trophy. He sits with Murphy perched on his shoulders while the rest of the boys crowd in on either side. Uncle Rudy stands next to his team with a smile on his face that must make his cheeks hurt.

The picture doesn't show it, but close by Mom, Chas and Bernie are leaping and screaming so much that their throats are going to hurt for days.

Sylvia Olsen has many sources of inspiration for her children's writing. Her mother and mother-in-law have more than two hundred grandchildren and great-grandchildren between them! Sylvia has lived in the Tsartlip First Nation for almost thirty years. She works as a First Nation's community development consultant. Sylvia is the author of four other novels for children and teens: *No Time to Say Goodbye*, *The Girl With a Baby*, and *White Girl*, all published by Sono Nis Press, and *Catching Spring*, published by Orca. *Murphy and Mousetrap* is her second book with Orca.